Karen's Angel

**Look for these
and other books about Karen in the
Baby-sitters Little Sister series**

BABY-SITTERS

Little Sister

Karen's Angel

Ann M. Martin

Illustrations by Susan Tang

A
LITTLE APPLE
PAPERBACK

SCHOLASTIC INC.
New York Toronto London Auckland Sydney

The author gratefully acknowledges
Stephanie Calmenson
for her help
with this book.

ISBN 0-590-26025-1

Copyright © 1995 by Ann M. Martin. All rights reserved. Published by Scholastic Inc. BABY-SITTERS LITTLE SISTER, APPLE PAPERBACKS, and the APPLE PAPERBACKS logo are registered trademarks of Scholastic Inc.

12 11 10 9 8 7 6 5 4 3 2 1   5 6 7 8 9/9 0/0

Printed in the U.S.A.   40

First Scholastic printing, December 1995

1

Karen's Collection

"It is almost time to say good-bye, Emily Junior," I said. "You will be away for two whole months."

It was the end of November. I was at the little house talking to my pet rat. I named my rat after my sister, Emily Michelle. I will tell you more about my sister later. But first, I will tell you about me.

I am Karen Brewer. I am seven years old. I have blonde hair, blue eyes, and some freckles. I wear glasses. I wear my blue pair for reading. I wear my pink pair the rest of the time. (I do not wear any glasses when I am taking a bath or sleeping.) I have a little brother named Andrew. He is four going on five.

Do you want to know where Emily Junior is going? I will tell you. She is going with me to my other house. You see, Andrew and I have two houses — a little house and a big house. We switch houses every month. Only this time we will do something different. We will stay at the big house for two months — December and January. (That is a special arrangement Mommy and Daddy made. It has something to do with the holidays, but I forget what.)

Speaking of holidays, Thanksgiving just ended a few days ago. It was really fun. Now Christmas is coming. I can hardly wait! It has been a very long time since Andrew and I spent more than a few days at the big house in December. This year we are going to be there for *all* of Christmas. We do not even have to leave when it is over. I know Christmastime will be exciting. Exciting things always happen at the big house.

"I hope you will not miss me too much, Goosie," I said to my stuffed cat. "You will have plenty of company here. And you know I will come back. I always do."

I wiped a pretend tear from Goosie's cheek. He always gets sad when I tell him I am going. But he is fine once I leave. I know because Mommy checks on Goosie for me.

Aside from Emily Junior, I do not have to take much with me to the big house. That is because I already have lots of things there. I looked around my room to see if there was anything special I wanted to take this time. Of course there was! My angel collection. I started it a little while ago. I did not want to forget it. Especially at Christmas.

You see, I love angels. They are special and magical. I want to have as many as I can. And I want to know as much as I can

3

about them. Here is what I have in my collection so far: An angel mug. A very good book called *My Book of Angels*. A postcard with an angel on it from my pen pal, Maxie, in New York. (She got it at a store called Everything Angels. Some day I will go there.) My angel rubber stamp. And a pipe cleaner angel I made at school. It is a gigundoly beautiful collection.

I think I will make tags shaped like angels to put on my gifts this year. I will need a lot of tags because I have a lot of gifts to give. That is what happens when you have two houses and two families.

Did I tell you yet how I got to have two houses and two families? I do not think so. I will tell you right now.

Hooray for Being a Two-Two

Are you ready? Here is the story of how I got to have two houses and two families. The story starts a long time ago.

When I was little, I lived in one big house in Stoneybrook, Connecticut, with Mommy, Daddy, and Andrew. Then Mommy and Daddy started fighting a lot. They explained to Andrew and me that they loved us very much, but they could not get along with each other anymore. So they got a divorce.

After the divorce, Mommy moved with

Andrew and me to a little house not far away. She met a very nice man named Seth. Mommy and Seth got married. That is how Seth became my stepfather. So this is who lives at the little house: Mommy, Seth, Andrew, me, Rocky (Seth's cat), Midgie (Seth's dog), Emily Junior, and Bob (Andrew's hermit crab).

Daddy stayed at the big house after the divorce. (It is the house he grew up in.) He met someone nice, too. Her name is Elizabeth. She and Daddy got married. That is how Elizabeth became my stepmother.

Elizabeth was married before and has four children. They are Kristy, who is thirteen and the best stepsister ever; David Michael, who is seven like me; and Sam and Charlie, who are so old they are in high school.

I already told you I have a sister named Emily. But I did not tell you that she is two and a half and was adopted from a faraway place called Vietnam. I love Emily a lot. That is why I named my rat after her.

Another person I love a lot is my step-grandmother, Nannie. Nannie is Elizabeth's mother. She came to the big house to help take care of Emily. But really she helps take care of everyone.

Now I will tell you about the pets at the big house. They are Shannon, David Michael's big Bernese mountain dog puppy; Boo-Boo, Daddy's cranky old tabby cat; Crystal Light the Second, my goldfish; and Goldfishie, Andrew's chimpanzee. (Just kidding!) Oh, yes. Emily Junior and Bob live at the big house whenever Andrew and I are there.

Remember I said I did not have to take much to the big house? That is because Andrew and I have two of lots of different things. We keep one of each thing at each house. That way we do not have to carry so much back and forth when we switch. I have a special name for Andrew and me. I call us Andrew Two-Two and Karen Two-Two. (I got that name from a book my teacher read at school. It is called *Jacob Two-*

Two Meets the Hooded Fang.) Andrew and I have two mommies and two daddies, two houses and two families, two cats and two dogs.

Here are some other things we each have two of. We have two sets of toys, clothes, and books. I have two bicycles. Andrew has two tricycles. I have two stuffed cats. Goosie lives at the little house. Moosie lives at the big house. I have two pieces of Tickly, my special blanket. And I have two best friends. Nancy Dawes lives next door to the little house. Hannie Papadakis lives across the street and one house over from the big house. Nancy and Hannie and I are in the same second-grade class at Stoneybrook Academy. (We call ourselves the Three Musketeers. That is because we like to do everything together.)

This year I will have two Christmases. I will have a little-house Christmas and a big-house Christmas. Hooray for being a two-two!

Big-House Greetings

It was Friday, the first of December. I woke up and got dressed at the little house. I went to school with Nancy on the little-house school bus. But when school was over, I took the big-house school bus home with Hannie.

My month at the little house was over. Two months at the big house were beginning.

"See you tomorrow!" I called to Hannie when we reached our street.

I raced to Daddy's house. Nannie was

waiting for me at the door. She had a big smile on her face.

"Come in!" she said. "Emily Junior is upstairs in your room. Emily Michelle and Andrew are in the kitchen. And I have a snack ready for you."

Nannie had picked Andrew up from preschool. Then she picked up Emily Junior and Bob from the little house.

I kissed Nannie hello. Then I raced into the kitchen to say hello to Emily Michelle and Andrew. I hugged Emily. (I did not hug Andrew since I had just seen him in the morning.) Then I ran to the office to hug Daddy. I did not stay long. I did not want to bother him while he was working.

"I will be right back," I told Nannie.

I ran upstairs to make sure Emily Junior was okay. (She was.) Then I unpacked my angel collection and set it on my dresser. I did not want my angels to be in a dark knapsack any longer than they had to. Angels are probably happy wherever they are. But I did not want to take chances.

After I washed up, I went back to the kitchen to have my snack. Nannie had made cinnamon toast with cream cheese, and hot chocolate to drink. Yum.

While we were eating, Kristy walked in.

"Welcome back!" she said. "I am happy to see you. I missed you guys."

(I told you she is the best stepsister ever.)

Then David Michael came running in.

"Hi, Karen. Hi, Andrew," he said. He dropped his book bag and grabbed a piece of cinnamon toast.

"Please wash your hands," said Nannie.

After I ate my snack, I visited with Kristy, checked on Crystal Light, and did my homework. Before I knew it, Sam, Charlie, and Elizabeth had returned home. Elizabeth gave Andrew and me great big hugs. She was gigundoly happy to see us. Everyone was.

"Are you ready for a big-house Christmas?" asked Elizabeth.

"I am ready!" I said.

The Christmas spirit was already in the air. Sam was humming "Jingle Bells." David Michael was telling Christmas jokes. My whole big-house family was in an extra good mood.

At dinnertime, the ten of us sat down around the table to eat. Big-house meals are always noisy and fun.

"We should get our tree early this year," Charlie said to Daddy. "The best ones go fast."

"We need to buy plenty of wrapping paper this year," Kristy said to David Michael.

"You are right," David Michael replied. "Last year we almost ran out."

Sam and Elizabeth talked about decorations. Nannie said something about the cookies she and Emily were going to bake. It sounded as though everyone already had an important Christmas job to do. Everyone except Andrew and me.

"What about us?" I said. "Do we have a job?"

Daddy and Elizabeth gave each other funny looks. I think they had forgotten about us.

"We are sorry," said Elizabeth. "You have not been with us much at Christmastime. So we did not think of a job for you yet. We will think of one very soon."

"All the important jobs are taken," I said.

"Do not worry," said Daddy. "I promise we will find an important job for you and Andrew."

I hoped so. Important jobs are my favorite kind.

4

Holiday Surprises

"Good morning, class," said Ms. Colman. "Please take your seats. Karen, would you take attendance for us? Afterward, I have an announcement to make."

"Sure!" I replied.

Monday morning was off to a great start. It was my turn to take attendance. And Ms. Colman had a Surprising Announcement. (I love Surprising Announcements!)

I checked off each name as fast as I could. First I found my own name in the book. Check. I found Hannie's and Nancy's names next. Check, check. I looked around to see who else was present.

I sit at the front of the room because I wear glassses. Ms. Colman says it is easier to see from there. The other glasses-wearers who sit up front with me are Ricky Torres and Natalie Springer. (Ricky is my pretend husband. We got married on the playground at recess one day.) Ricky and Natalie were both there. Check, check.

Addie Sidney was present. (She was busy peeling Thanksgiving stickers off her wheelchair tray. She had a package of new holiday stickers waiting to replace them.) Check. Pamela Harding, my best enemy, was present. Check. So were her friends Leslie Morris and Jannie Gilbert. Check, check. Bobby Gianelli was present. (He used to be a bully. But he is not so much of a bully anymore.) Check. Terry and Tami Barkan were there. (They are twins.) Check, check. Audrey Green was there. Check. Hank Reubens was there. Check. I checked off a few more names. Then I was done.

"Everyone is here," I said. "We are ready for the announcement."

"Thank you, Karen," replied Ms. Colman. "Last month you all made beautiful Thanksgiving decorations for Stoneybrook Manor. Everyone there loved them. This month, you have been invited to make new holiday decorations. And you have been invited to put up the decorations yourselves."

Yippee! This was a great announcement. I am very good at making decorations. I love field trips. And I like to visit the people who live at Stoneybrook Manor. (They are older people who cannot take care of themselves at home anymore.) I was sure they would want to tell us in person how much they loved our decorations. And I would be happy to listen.

The holidays were looking better and better every day.

School was fun. The day passed quickly. On the way home, Hannie had an announcement of her own to make.

"I am glad you will be at the big house for the holidays this year, Karen," she said. "Now you can be in our Christmas pageant."

"Your what?" I asked.

"Our Christmas pageant," Hannie replied. "Every year the kids in the neighborhood get together to put on a pageant for our families and neighbors. It is a really big deal. We do it at my house. We turn the dining room into a stage. The sliding doors make great curtains. We have props and costumes and everything."

"It sounds like fun," I said.

"It is. Everyone looks forward to it. Now you and Andrew can be in it, too," said Hannie.

"Thanks," I replied.

We had reached our stop, so I had to say good-bye to Hannie. She promised to tell me more about the pageant later that afternoon.

I was surprised that Hannie had not mentioned it to me before. I had been missing out on all the fun. Oh, well. At least Andrew and I would get to be part of it this year. Better late than never.

5

Casting Call

After school, I ate a snack with David Michael and Andrew. Then it was time to go to Hannie's house. She had called a meeting for everyone who wanted to be in the Christmas pageant. (I guess Hannie was going to be in charge of the pageant this year. Maybe I could be in charge another year.)

David Michael had been in the pageant before and wanted to be in it again. Andrew wanted to be in it, too. So the three of us went across the street together. I knocked on the door. Linny answered it. (Linny is Hannie's brother. He is nine going on ten.)

"Come in," he said. "We have been waiting for you."

The living room was filled with kids from the neighborhood. They were Scott Hsu, who is seven and Hannie's pretend husband; Timmy Hsu, who is five; Callie and Keith Bates, who are four-year-old twins; and Maria Kilbourne, who is eight.

"Attention, everyone," said Hannie. "I know some of you are here for the first time. So I will explain everything as we go along."

I watched Hannie lead the meeting. I felt bad that I was not in charge. But only a little bit. After all, Hannie is a Musketeer. The Three Musketeers' motto is one for all and all for one.

"We are going to put on the story of the Nativity, just like last year," said Hannie. "We will need to cast the parts of Joseph, Mary, the three Wise Men, the angel, some shepherds, and some animals."

I raised my hand to ask a question. I did not want to interrupt Hannie while she was talking.

"Yes, Karen?" said Hannie.

"How will we decide who gets which part? Will we draw straws or something?" I asked.

"I have already assigned the parts. It took me a long time, but I think you will all be happy," replied Hannie. "I will tell you which parts you are playing as soon as I find my list. I know I have it here somewhere."

Hannie looked in all her pockets. Finally she pulled a crumpled paper from the back pocket of her jeans.

She read out the parts: Andrew and Callie were playing the animals. Timmy and Maria were shepherds. Linny, David Michael, and Keith were the three Wise Men. Scott was Joseph. Hannie was the angel.

"Baby Jesus will be played by one of my dolls. And I want Karen to have the part of Mary," said Hannie.

22

"Hey, how come?" asked Linny. "That is supposed to be your part. You play Mary every year."

"This is Karen's first year in the pageant," said Hannie. "I want her to have this important role."

Hannie smiled at me. I smiled back. But I was not happy. I did not want to be Mary. I was *dying* to play the angel. It was the only part I truly wanted. The angel would get to wear wings and a halo. I would give anything to switch parts with Hannie.

But I could not say so. Hannie was being nice to me. I decided that even though I was not going to play the angel, I had to act like one.

I smiled at Hannie and did not say a word.

6

An Important Job

"**A**ttention, everyone," said Daddy. "Elizabeth and I have decided on a job for Andrew and Karen. It is a very important job indeed."

"Hooray!" I said. "What is it?"

We were at the dinner table. My big-house family was all ears. They wanted to hear about our new job.

"Well, we usually have a star at the top of the Christmas tree," said Elizabeth. "But our star is so old it is falling apart. We thought it would be nice to have an angel on the tree this year. Your job is to find one."

"Wow! I know everything about angels," I replied.

"My teacher says I am an angel sometimes," said Andrew.

"Your teacher is right," said Charlie. "But you are too heavy to sit on top of the tree."

While everyone was laughing at Charlie's joke, I was thinking. Thinking about our job of finding the angel. It really *was* an important job.

"You do not have to look so serious," whispered Sam. "It is not your job to find a *real* angel."

"I know that," I replied.

"You know, there are no such things as angels," said Sam.

"Well, I like to think there are," I replied.

After dinner, I called a meeting. It was only a little meeting for Andrew and me. But at least I was in charge.

"We need to decide what kind of angel

we want. Should we make one, or buy one? Whatever we do, the angel must be really terrific," I said.

"I do not know what kind it should be," said Andrew.

"I have a very good book we can look at," I replied. "Maybe we will find an angel we like there."

We carefully looked through *My Book of Angels.* That did not help, because we liked every angel we saw.

"I will get more books at school tomorrow," I said. "Maybe we will see the perfect angel in one of them."

At recess the next day, I went to the library instead of the playground. I asked Mr. Counts, the school librarian, for books with pictures of angels.

"We have several good ones, Karen," he replied. "I will help you find them."

I took out four books, which is the most we are allowed to borrow. Then I went to see Mr. Mackey, the art teacher.

"Do you have any books about making angels?" I asked.

"There are some excellent craft books on my shelves over there. Feel free to browse and borrow," Mr. Mackey replied.

I browsed and borrowed two books. At home, I called another meeting. I opened the new books to the pictures of my favorite angels.

"Okay," I said. "It is time to decide. When I count to three, point to the angel you like the best. One, two, three!"

Guess what! Andrew and I pointed to the same one. It was amazing. I was sure it was an angel's magic sign. The angel we picked was wearing a blue flowing robe. She had a golden halo and golden wings. She was blowing on a silver trumpet. She was fantastic.

Then I remembered something. I saw an angel just like her in the Connecticut Yankee Gift Shop downtown. (I am always on the lookout for angels.)

"Go get your money, Andrew. I will get mine. We will see how much we have," I said.

I counted our money. It was just enough to buy the angel.

"Let's ask Daddy if he will drive us downtown on Saturday," I said.

Daddy said he would be glad to. Yippee!

7

Oops!

"Are you ready to go?" asked Daddy.

"We are ready!" I said.

It was Saturday morning. Daddy was driving Andrew and me downtown. Kristy was coming, too. She wanted to buy wrapping paper and ribbon at the card shop, since she was in charge of wrapping gifts with David Michael. The card shop was next door to the Connecticut Yankee Gift Shop.

When we reached the gift shop, I said, "We would like to go in by ourselves. We want our angel to be a surprise. No one is allowed to see her until Christmas Eve when we put her on the tree."

"I do not like letting you and your brother go into a store alone," said Daddy.

"It is a small store," I replied. "We will not get lost or anything. Really."

"Are you sure you do not need my help?" asked Daddy.

"We are sure," I replied.

"All right. Just stay inside," said Daddy. "We will come back to get you in ten minutes."

"Thank you, Daddy!" I said. I opened the door to the store. Tiny bells tinkled above our heads when we walked inside.

"May I help you with something?" asked the store owner.

"No, thank you," I replied.

I knew just where to find the angels. They were at the back of the store. I led Andrew there.

"I see her! I see our angel," said Andrew, pointing to the shelf where she sat.

"She is the most beautiful angel of all,"

I replied. I reached up and carefully carried her down. A price tag was hanging from her halo. Uh-oh. She was a little more expensive than I remembered. Ten dollars more, to be exact.

"What is wrong?" asked Andrew.

"I thought this angel cost nine dollars. But now I see there is a number one before the number nine. That means she is nineteen dollars. We do not have enough money to buy her," I said. "We have to put her back."

Andrew looked sad. "Let me just see her first," he said. He held out his hands.

I am not sure what happened next. Either I let go too fast, or Andrew did not hold her tightly enough. All I know was the angel fell to the floor and broke into pieces.

Oops.

"What is going on back there?" called the store owner. He rushed to the back of the store where Andrew and I stood staring at what was left of the angel.

"We are sorry," I said. "It was an accident."

The store owner was red in the face.

"That may be," he said. "But you will still have to pay for it."

He pointed to a sign on the wall. It said: *If you break it, you own it.*

I reached into my pocket and handed over our money.

"That is all we have," I said.

"Well, you will just have to owe me the rest," said the store owner.

He told us exactly how much that would be.

"We cannot give it to you right away," I said. "But I promise we will have the money for you by Christmas Eve."

"I would like your parents' names and their phone number. Just in case," said the store owner.

We followed him to the counter where he wrote everything down. Andrew looked scared. I thought he was going to cry.

When the store owner was finished, we waited inside the entrance for Daddy and Kristy. As soon as we saw them coming, we rushed outside.

"Did you get it?" asked Kristy.

"No, we did not buy it after all," I replied quickly. "Can we go home now, Daddy? I am hungry."

I was not really hungry. I just wanted to get as far away from the Connecticut Yankee Gift Shop as I could.

Holiday Helpers

"Psst. Andrew. Meeting in my room," I whispered when we returned to the house.

We went to my room and closed the door.

"We are in big trouble. We have no angel. And we do not have a single cent between us," I said. "We cannot buy another angel. We cannot even buy Christmas presents. And we have to pay the store owner the money we owe him by Christmas Eve."

"I guess we messed up," said Andrew.

"We sure did. Big time," I replied. "We

had one little responsibility and we blew it."

"We could make an angel," said Andrew.

"Maybe. But a fancy store-bought angel would be much better. We need to earn some money," I said. "Then our troubles will be over."

"How will we do that?" asked Andrew.

"I have an idea," I replied. "Everyone is complaining about how busy they are. They are saying they do not have enough time to get everything done before Christmas. We will help them."

"And they will pay us!" said Andrew.

"Exactly," I replied. "We need to get organized. First we should make uniforms. That way we will look like serious workers."

"I want to wear a fireman uniform," said Andrew.

"That is not the kind of uniform I mean," I said. "We have to make a uniform to go with our business."

"Does our business have a name?" asked Andrew.

I thought and thought. Finally, I came up with a name. I thought of a very good motto, too.

"We will call ourselves the Holiday Helpers. Our motto will be: 'If you have a job that needs to be done, ask Holiday Helpers and you'll be free to have fun.'"

"I like that!" said Andrew.

"Thank you," I replied. "We will charge fifty cents for each job we do. Come on. Let's make our uniforms."

I got out paper, crayons, glitter, string, and glue. We made signs that said: Holiday Helpers, 50¢ a job. We hung the signs around our necks with string. Then we stood in front of the mirror to admire ourselves. The Holiday Helpers were ready.

We knocked on Nannie's door first.

"Holiday Helpers to the rescue," I said.

Then Andrew and I said together, "If you have a job that needs to be done, ask Holiday Helpers and you'll be free to have fun."

Nannie smiled. "I certainly could use some help. Would the Holiday Helpers be able to dust this room?"

"We are very good dusters," I said. "When you come back, the job will be done."

"Thank you," replied Nannie.

When we finished dusting, we found our next customer. It was Kristy. (She liked our motto a lot.)

"I lost one of my high-top sneakers," said Kristy. "I have been looking for it all morning."

"Holiday Helpers to the rescue!" I said.

Andrew found the sneaker under a poster that had fallen off the wall.

Daddy and Elizabeth asked us to read to Emily before her nap.

David Michael hired us to brush Shannon.

Charlie asked us to wipe the windows on

the Junk Bucket. (That is what we call his car.)

Sam asked us to take phone messages for him while he went downtown to buy batteries for his radio.

Everyone paid us promptly. But by the end of the day, we still did not have much money.

"We only have three dollars," I said. "I think we charged too little."

We could not go back and ask for more money. That would not be nice. But I did not give up hope. Things would work out somehow. They always did.

9

Holiday Spirit

I put my money worries aside when I arrived at school on Monday. Ms. Colman said we would spend the afternoon making our holiday decorations for Stoneybrook Manor. It was hard to worry and have fun at the same time.

We did our schoolwork in the morning. After recess, we found arts-and-crafts supplies set out around our room.

"If you need any help, just let me know," said Ms. Colman.

I moved to the back to sit with Hannie and Nancy.

"I am going to make a Christmas tree," I said. "What are you going to make?"

"I am going to make a diorama of Santa flying through the sky in his sleigh," replied Hannie.

"I will make a cardboard dreidel," said Nancy.

"Can I play the dreidel game with you?" I asked.

"Sure," replied Nancy.

Nancy once showed me how to play the dreidel game. It is part of the Hanukkah holiday. A dreidel is a top with letters on each side. You spin the top, then do different things, depending on which letter comes up when the top stops. You even win little prizes. It is fun.

"I will be right back," I said.

I looked in the supply closet for a few more things. I wanted my Christmas tree to have very interesting ornaments. I needed a little of everything I could find.

Except for the glitter. I needed a lot of that.

"Is there any more glitter in there?" asked Sara Ford.

I had filled my cup to the very top. The jar was almost empty. It was time to show some holiday spirit.

"Here, you can have some of this," I said.

"Thank you," replied Sara. "I am making a mkeka mat out of newspaper. I want to decorate it with glitter. I think that will look very nice at Stoneybrook Manor, don't you?"

"It will look great," I replied.

A real mkeka mat from Africa is made out of straw. It is one of the gifts given during the Kwanza holiday. That is the holiday that Sara, Ms. Colman, and Omar Harris celebrate.

When Sara left, I turned back to my supplies. The next thing I knew, Pamela was there.

"Hi, Karen," she said. "I need a sheet of blue construction paper. Have you seen any?"

I happened to know that I had taken the last sheet.

Pamela looked through the closet. Then she looked at me. She saw the blue construction paper poking out from my supplies.

"I guess I could take white paper and color it with a blue crayon," said Pamela.

Hmm. Pamela is usually my best enemy. But she was trying to be nice. She was showing holiday spirit. I decided to show some holiday spirit right back. (I did not want my best enemy to have more holiday spirit than me.)

"You can have half of this sheet," I said.

"Hey, thanks," replied Pamela. (She looked surprised.)

We cut the paper in half. I grabbed a few more things from the closet, then raced back to my desk. It was time to get to work.

By the end of the afternoon, I had made the most beautiful tree ever. Hannie's diorama looked so real I thought I heard sleigh bells ringing. Nancy's dreidel spun

44

like a real top you would find in a store.

"You have all done a wonderful job," said Ms. Colman. "Next Tuesday we will visit Stoneybrook Manor."

I could hardly wait. We had beautiful decorations and lots of holiday spirit to share.

Making Costumes

On Wednesday after school the kids in the Christmas pageant gathered at Hannie's house.

"We are going to start making our costumes today," said Hannie. "Linny and I were sure we put away a box of things last year. But we cannot find them. So we have to start all over."

"Sari help," said Hannie's little sister. (Sari is two and a half, like Emily.)

"You can help me with my angel costume," said Hannie.

I wished I were making the angel costume. That would be exciting. The costume for Mary was not as much fun. I could wear the long-sleeved white blouse I had on. And Mrs. Papadakis lent me one of her skirts. It came down to my ankles. She gave me a light blue shawl to wear around my shoulders and a scarf to put on my head. On the day of the pageant I would wear my black party shoes instead of sneakers. That was it. I was done.

"You look great," said Hannie.

"Thanks," I replied. "I will help Andrew with his costume now."

Andrew's costume was a little more exciting. He was going to be one of the lambs in the barn where Jesus was born. He needed to be white and fluffy.

I found cotton puffs in a jar in the Papadakises' bathroom. I helped Andrew stick them together with glue.

"We need a little bit of glue right here," I said, pointing to a couple of cotton puffs.

Andrew squeezed the bottle of glue hard.

Sticky white paste squirted out.

"We only needed a *little* glue," I said.

Luckily the glue dried fast. The cotton puffs felt a little stiff. But they looked okay. We glued together a whole bunch of them and put them on Andrew's head. Now all he needed was white clothes.

"Maa-aa. Maa-aa," said Andrew.

He looked and sounded like a perfect little lamb.

I had already finished making two costumes. Hannie and Sari were still working on the angel costume. Sari held up a wire hanger that was bent in the shape of a wing. Hannie was covering it with some white material Mrs. Papadakis had found in her sewing basket. It made a beautiful angel's wing. I wished it were my beautiful angel's wing.

I felt someone tugging on my shawl. It was Callie.

"Will you help me look like a lamb, too?" she said.

"Sure," I replied.

I handed Callie the container of glue. Out of the corner of my eye, I watched Hannie making her second angel wing.

"Squeeze," I said.

Callie squeezed hard just the way Andrew had squeezed. Glue squirted out again. Why do little kids do that? I guess they do not know any better.

When we got tired of working on our costumes, we started on the announcement fliers. Mrs. Papadakis typed the words we asked for on her computer. Then she printed them on paper. The fliers said:

Hear ye, hear ye.
Come one, come all to
our famous Christmas Pageant.
Time: Saturday, December 23rd at 7pm
Place: the Papadakis house

We sat down with green and red markers and drew beautiful holiday borders on the tliers. When we were done we had enough for our families and a few left over to post in the neighborhood.

Getting ready for a Christmas pageant is gigundoly fun!

11

Christmas in the Air

Mommy. Check. Daddy. Check. Seth. Check. Elizabeth. Check. Kristy. Check.

It was Saturday morning. I was not taking attendance. I was in my room checking off my gift list. Before Andrew and I broke the angel, I had gifts for about half the people on my list. There were still a lot of names to go.

"I do not have money left to buy anything," I said to Moosie. "So I better get busy making gifts."

All I had to do was think of what to make.

I decided to go downstairs and see what everyone was up to. Maybe I would get some ideas. Maybe I would also get some lunch. I was hungry.

I took a pencil and paper with me. That way if I got any great gift ideas, I could write them down.

I was halfway down the stairs when David Michael raced past me.

"Excuse me!" he said.

He was hiding something under his shirt.

"What is that?" I asked.

"Nothing you need to know about. At least not yet," he said, smiling. He disappeared into his room.

Hmm. Mysterious.

When I reached the bottom of the stairs, I was practically knocked over by Kristy.

"Sorry," she said.

Kristy was hiding something under her shirt, too.

Aha! I did not even have to ask what it was. I knew. Kristy and David Michael were hiding presents under their shirts.

They were running upstairs to wrap them.

Ooh. Things were getting exciting.

When Kristy passed by me, I noticed that one of her shoelaces was torn. I wrote "shoelaces" on my gift list next to Kristy's name. I happened to have a brand-new package of shoelaces that I had not opened yet. That could be one of my gifts to Kristy.

Ding-dong. The doorbell rang. I was just in time to answer it. I looked outside and saw Mr. Venta, the mail carrier. I opened the door for him. (I am allowed to open the door for Mr. Venta.)

"I have a package addressed to your dad," he said.

In a flash, Daddy was behind me.

"Thank you, Mr. Venta. I will take that," he said.

It was a very interesting box. It was decorated with red and white candy cane stripes. A drawing of a Christmas wreath was on the address label. It looked as if it might be a present. But I did not get to look at it for very long. Daddy excused himself and disappeared upstairs. It was another mystery package. I wondered who it was for.

My tummy was making rumbling noises. It was time for lunch. I hurried into the kitchen. Nannie was taking some leftovers out of the oven. I noticed that her potholder was old and torn.

A new potholder would be easy for me to make. I wrote "potholder" on the list next to Nannie's name.

"Would you set the table, please, Karen?" asked Nannie. "There is a new package of napkins on the counter."

The napkins were decorated with red bells and green holly. Christmas was coming to the big house.

I did not have an angel for the tree. I was not playing the angel in the pageant. I owed a store owner money that I did not have. But I was still happy. Presents were being wrapped. Napkins had holly on them. Christmas was in the air!

12

Christmas Countdown

I woke up on Sunday and looked at my calendar. It was December 17th. That meant eight more days to Christmas.

I found Nannie, Elizabeth, Kristy, Emily, David Michael, Andrew, and Sam in the kitchen eating breakfast.

"Hi, everyone. Where are Daddy and Charlie?" I asked.

"They are on a secret mission," replied Sam.

"They will be home soon," said Elizabeth. "You will know where they have been as soon as they walk through the door."

I ate my favorite breakfast of Krispy Krunchy cereal. Nannie made me a cup of hot chocolate to go with it.

I was not sure what to do next. There were so many choices. I could make gifts for Hannie and Nancy. I could figure out what to do about getting an angel. I could decorate my room for Christmas.

"Karen, would you like to help Emily and me bake Christmas cookies this morning?" asked Nannie.

That was it! I could help Nannie and Emily bake Christmas cookies.

"Yes!" I said. "What kind will we make?"

"Ginger cookies and sugar cookies," said Nannie.

"Yum and yum," I replied.

My first job was to beat the eggs. While I was working, a Christmas song came on the radio. I sang along. *It's beginning to look a lot like Christmas!"*

Then I made up my own words.

There are presents hidden everywhere.
It's beginning to feel a lot like Christmas.
You will soon be smelling cookies in the air!

When the dough was ready, Nannie let me use the Christmas cookie cutters. They were shaped like trees and stars.

We had just popped the first batch of cookies into the oven when Daddy and Charlie came home. They were carrying a great big tree tied up with rope.

"You bought a Christmas tree! That was your secret mission," I said.

We helped them carry the tree into the living room.

"We think we got a good one this year," said Daddy.

He cut the rope off. The branches dropped down.

"It is so big," said Kristy.

"And it is not one bit lopsided," I said.

"It is an amazing tree," said Elizabeth.

"Thank you, everyone, thank you," said Charlie.

I wanted to decorate the tree right away. But we were going to save that job for Christmas Eve. So I spent the day baking cookies, making gifts, and listening to Kristy read stories from a very good book called *Children of Christmas*.

The next day when I returned from school, Sam was stringing up lights outside. Elizabeth came home from work early to help Sam decorate the house inside and out. (That was their job.)

By the time they finished, it was dark. Elizabeth called, "Come outside and look, everyone."

My big-house family put on jackets and stood together in the yard. Sam flipped a switch. The Christmas lights flashed on. A wreath hung on the door. Red candles stood tall in the windows. Tinsel hung down around them. Our house was glowing.

I felt a tug on my jacket. It was Andrew.

"Hey, Karen," he whispered. "What are

we going to do about the angel? We have to get one. It is our job."

Andrew sounded worried. I was not in the mood to worry with him. I was too happy.

"It is okay. We have time," I replied.

It was December 18th. There were seven days till Christmas. Seven more days to worry about an angel.

13

Stoneybrook Manor

"Knock, knock," I said.

"Who's there?" replied Hannie.

"Sandy," I said.

"Sandy who?" said Nancy.

"Sandy Claus is coming to town!"

It was Tuesday afternoon. My classmates and I were riding the school bus to Stoneybrook Manor. Ms. Colman had packed up the decorations we had made. We were going to hang them up and spend the rest of the afternoon visiting the people there.

The first time we went to Stoneybrook

Manor I had felt nervous. Lots of kids had. But no one felt nervous anymore. Now we knew the people there. Many of them were our friends.

When we arrived, Mrs. Fellows greeted us. Mrs. Fellows helps run Stoneybrook Manor.

"Welcome, children," she said. "Everyone is looking forward to seeing you. Please come in."

I saw a Christmas tree inside. But it was kind of sad looking. It was not nearly as pretty as the Christmas tree at the big house. The place needed some cheering up.

I took out the paper tree I had made. It was small. But it was cheerful.

"May I see that?" asked a lady I had not met before.

"Sure," I said. "I made the whole tree and every one of the ornaments myself."

"It is beautiful," said the lady.

"My name is Karen Brewer. What is your name?" I asked.

The lady stopped smiling. She looked confused. And unhappy. I was sorry I had asked her name.

"It is okay," I said. "You do not have to tell me your name. It could be your secret."

Mrs. Fellows hurried to us.

"This is Mrs. Humphrey. She has trouble remembering things sometimes," she said.

I decided I would not ask any more questions. I did not want Mrs. Humphrey to feel unhappy. I told Mrs. Humphrey all about myself instead. Mrs. Humphrey was happy to listen. I made her laugh a lot. We were having a very good time.

Nancy was visiting with Grandma B. The first time we visited Stoneybrook Manor, some of us adopted grandparents. Grandma B. was my adopted grandma. But I gave her to Nancy because I have four grandmas already.

Nancy and Grandma B. were playing with the dreidel Nancy had made. They were singing a Hanukkah song together.

Oh, dreidel, dreidel, dreidel,
I made it out of clay.
And when it's dried and ready,
Then dreidel I will play!

Hannie was showing her diorama to a nice man I had seen before. He had bright blue eyes and snow-white hair. Then Hannie said something and the man laughed. (Maybe she told him my knock-knock joke.)

In between visiting, we hung up our decorations. When we finished, the room looked a whole lot better.

"It is time for refreshments," said Mrs. Fellows.

She brought out cookies and punch for everyone. We sang holiday songs. Then Mrs. Fellows made a speech.

"Thank you for coming today. It cheers us up greatly to see your happy faces. And we will enjoy the beautiful decorations you made."

The residents clapped for us. That made me feel good. Ms. Colman promised we would come again to visit in the spring. Then it was time to leave.

I said good-bye to Mrs. Humphrey. I even gave her a hug. I was happy to have a brand-new friend.

14

Dress Rehearsal

Now it was time to worry. It was Friday afternoon. There were only three more days till Christmas. Andrew and I still had not figured out what to do about getting an angel for the tree.

I did not feel like going to Hannie's house. But I had to. She had called for a dress rehearsal at two o'clock. (School was out for winter vacation.) The pageant would be held the next evening at seven.

I went to Hannie's in a grumpy mood. I did not feel like rehearsing because I was playing the part of Mary and not the angel. All I could think about were angels. Not about *being* an angel. Not about *having* an angel. About *breaking* an angel.

"Okay, take your places, everyone," said Hannie.

I walked straight to the wrong spot. That was because my mind was on something else. (It was on you-know-what.) Hannie reminded me where I was supposed to stand. She reminded me nicely. But I gave her a grumpy look anyway.

The angel was the first one to talk in the pageant. That meant Hannie got to be the angel *and* to talk first. This did not make me feel any better.

"This child of Mary shall be the Holy Spirit," said Hannie.

"Maa! Maa!" said Andrew.

"No, not yet!" said Hannie. "You are not supposed to say anything until we get to the barn."

Andrew had said his part way too soon. His part did not come until the middle of the pageant. I guess his mind was on the angel, too.

It was Scott's turn to speak next. He had the part of Joseph. But he forgot what to say. Hannie had to remind him.

Then it was my turn to speak.

"I am ready for the journey," I said. (At least I remembered my part.)

Next we had to walk to Bethlehem. On the way, Scott tripped over my shawl. It was dragging on the floor.

"Karen, please pick up the shawl. It is not yours and you should not get it dirty," said Hannie.

"I did not get it dirty. I am not the one who stepped on it. Scott did," I said. "If you are so worried about the shawl, wear it yourself. You should be Mary."

"Maybe I *should* be Mary. You are not acting like Mary at all. The *real* Mary would never sound so mean," said Hannie.

"Well, I do not *want* to be Mary," I replied. "I never did. I want to be the angel."

"You do?" asked Hannie. "Well, I want

to be Mary. I am always Mary."

We stopped snapping at each other. We decided then and there to switch parts. Hannie was going to play Mary. I was going to be the angel. We went to another room and switched costumes. I walked back into the dining room with a big smile on my face.

"We will start the rehearsal over from the beginning," said Hannie.

I knew the angel's lines by heart. Now I was the first to speak.

"This child of Mary shall be the Holy Spirit," I said.

Yes! I was the angel! Now I could look forward to being in the pageant.

The Christmas Pageant

The next night at six-thirty, Andrew, David Michael, and I put on our costumes and walked over to the Papadakises' house. Snow was gently falling. Holiday lights were shining up and down the street. It was gigundoly beautiful.

We were the first members of the cast to arrive. Hannie's dining room was all set for the pageant. The star that shined over Bethlehem was hanging from the ceiling. (It was made of tin foil.) There were curtains on the sliding doors. A cardboard manger with

Hannie's baby doll was hidden away in a corner of the room. (Her doll was the perfect baby Jesus.)

Ding-dong. The rest of the cast was arriving. Then the guests started to arrive. I felt as if I had butterflies in my stomach. I was surprised I was nervous. I knew my part very well. And I knew everyone in the audience. They were my family and friends. But being an angel is important. I wanted to be just right.

There were ten of us in the pageant, not counting Hannie's doll. That meant five families were coming. Other people from the neighborhood who saw our fliers had promised to come, too. Soon the room was filled with people.

We let Emily and Sari hand out the programs. (Mrs. Papadakis had made them as a surprise for us.) The names of the cast were listed in order of appearance. Guess whose name was first. Mine. The program said in bold letters:

Angel .... Karen Brewer

I was so proud! I stood tall and spread my wings as wide as they would go.

When everyone was seated or standing in a comfortable place, Hannie began the program.

"Welcome to our Christmas pageant," she said. "We hope you enjoy the show. Please stay for refreshments."

Mr. Papadakis dimmed the dining-room lights. I closed my eyes and made believe I had gone back in time to the night Jesus was born. I was so busy making believe that I forgot to start speaking.

"Ahem," said Hannie.

I opened my eyes. I was back in Hannie's dining room. I knew I was supposed to say something. But for a minute, I could not remember what. Then it came to me.

"This child of Mary shall be the Holy Spirit," I said loudly and clearly.

"Come, let us go to Bethlehem," said Scott.

"I am ready for the journey," said Hannie.

Everyone said their parts perfectly. (But Andrew's fluffy white cotton puffs had fallen off. He looked like a lamb that had been shaved. No one seemed to mind, though.)

We ended by singing "Silent Night." Then Mr. Papadakis turned out all the dining-room lights. Linny held a flashlight so it shone on the star over Bethlehem. Hannie said, "Merry Christmas, everyone."

The audience began clapping. Someone called out, "Bravo!" The ten of us stood in a line, holding hands under the shining tin star.

When the lights were turned on, Mrs. Papadakis invited everyone into the living room for refreshments.

Kristy hurried over to me.

"You were a terrific angel," she said.

"I am very proud of you kids," said Daddy.

Elizabeth took turns hugging Andrew, David Michael, and me. She was smiling, but her eyes looked a little teary. I think she was crying because she was happy.

I was happy, too. It was my first big-house Christmas pageant. And it was a big-house Christmas success.

16

The Truth

When I woke up the next morning, I jumped out of bed. I looked at my calendar. It said: Sunday. December 24th. Christmas Eve. I expected to see in tiny print: Karen Brewer, you do not have an angel!

Why had I waited so long to find an angel? I guess I thought someone would send Andrew and me some Christmas money early. Or that we would earn the money ourselves. I thought somehow Andrew and I would be able to buy a wonderful angel to put on our Christmas tree. I was wrong.

Knock, knock. Andrew was at my door. He looked sleepy. And worried.

"Karen, are we going to get an angel today?" he asked.

"I wish we could," I said. "But we have no money."

Uh-oh. I remembered something important. I had promised to pay back the store owner by Christmas Eve.

"Good morning, Karen. Good morning, Andrew," said Kristy. She hurried past my room with an armful of boxes.

"Come on, sleepyheads. Come join us," said Elizabeth. She had an armful of boxes, too.

My family was bringing boxes of ornaments downstairs from the attic. Christmas Eve was supposed to be one of the best days of the season. So far it felt like the worst.

Andrew and I went downstairs to eat breakfast. The boxes from the attic were spread across the living room.

"We have such great ornaments," said

Kristy. "I can hardly wait until tonight to decorate the tree."

"We have not seen the angel yet," said Charlie.

"I am sure that will be the best ornament of all," said Nannie.

That did it. I started to cry. Andrew did, too. We were crying so hard we could not even tell anyone what was wrong. Daddy put his arms around us.

"It is okay," he said. "I am sure whatever is wrong can be fixed."

"We will help you," said Elizabeth. "Just tell us why you are crying."

"It cannot be fixed," I said.

"It is broken. We broke it," added Andrew.

"What did you break?" asked Daddy.

Andrew and I stopped crying long enough to tell our family the story. We told them that the angel was dropped and broke into little pieces. We told them that the store owner wanted us to pay him back.

"I am sorry," I said. "We had an impor-

tant job and we did not do it."

"I am sorry, too," said Andrew.

"That is all right," said Daddy. "You did not mean to break the angel. These things happen. I will call the store owner and straighten everything out."

"You do not have to buy an angel," said Kristy. "You can make one."

"That is right," said Elizabeth. "We would love to have a homemade angel on the tree."

We heard Daddy talking to the store owner. He said we would be there in an hour to pay for the angel.

After he hung up he said to Andrew and me, "It is true that when you break something in a store, you should pay for it. So I will pay for the angel now, and I would like the two of you to pay me back when you can. Does that sound fair?"

Andrew and I agreed it was fair.

After breakfast, we drove downtown with Daddy to pay the store owner. Then we hurried home to make an angel.

"Hey, Andrew, I have an idea," I said. "We can use this pipe cleaner angel I made at school."

I showed him my angel. She was bent out of shape. With a little work we would be able to use her, though.

We fixed her up and brought her to the living room. But she looked shabby next to the other ornaments. Oh, well. She would have to do.

17

A Little-House Visit

*H*onk, honk.

"Come on, Andrew. Mommy is here," I said.

We ran out of the big house to greet Mommy.

Andrew and I were going to spend the afternoon at the little house with Mommy, Seth, Granny, and Grandad. (Granny and Grandad are Seth's parents. They were visiting from Nebraska.)

On the way to the little house, we told Mommy the story of the broken angel.

Mommy was glad we were not sad anymore. She reminded us that whenever we have a problem we cannot solve ourselves, we should talk about it with a grown-up we trust.

Before we knew it we had reached the little house. It was all dressed up for Christmas. Lights twinkled and a wreath hung on the door. I could see the Christmas tree through the window. It was smaller than the big-house tree, but very pretty.

"We waited for you and Andrew to trim the tree with us," said Mommy.

I knew we would not have to worry about an angel. We had bought a beautiful star for the top of the tree the year before.

When I ran inside, I saw presents under the tree. Some of the tags had my name on them!

Then I saw Granny and Grandad. They came out of their room with their arms open wide. Andrew and I ran to them for a four-way hug.

"Merry Christmas!" said Granny.

"Santa delivered my best present one day early," said Grandad.

"What present is that?" I asked.

"My grandchildren!" Grandad replied.

Just then Seth walked into the kitchen carrying a bag of groceries.

"Hi, kids," he said. "I am so happy you are here. I just bought chestnuts, popcorn, and eggnog for us."

We gave Seth hugs.

"Let's trim the tree with popcorn," I said.

"Good idea," said Seth.

Ding-dong. I looked out the window. Nancy was standing on the stoop. She was holding a silver cookie tin and a package wrapped with red paper and green ribbon.

"Merry Christmas," said Nancy when I opened the door.

"Come in," I said.

"The cookies are for your whole family," said Nancy. "The present is for you. Do you want to open it now?"

"Sure!" I replied.

I tore off the ribbon and paper. Inside

was a beautiful book. The book was like a photo album with pockets to keep pictures in.

"This is so cool!" I said. "Thank you."

"Hello, Nancy," said Mommy. "Would you like to stay and help us trim the tree?"

"Yes," replied Nancy. "I just have to call my house to see if it is okay."

Nancy's mommy said she could stay. So we spent the afternoon eating chestnuts, drinking eggnog, and trimming the tree. We strung some of the popcorn and hung it on the branches. We ate the rest.

We hung almost all the ornaments. We saved the star for last. Seth stepped on a ladder and put it at the top.

"Everyone stand in front of the tree so I can take your picture," he said.

The six of us stood together and said, "Cheese!"

"I will put this picture in my new book," I said.

The afternoon was so much fun. But it

went too fast. Before I knew it, we were saying our good-byes and heading back to the big house.

"Merry Christmas, kids," said Mommy when she dropped us off. "I love you!"

18

Christmas Eve

When we walked into the big house, it was nice and warm. I smelled turkey and sweet potatoes cooking. Mmm.

"Did you have fun at the little house?" asked Kristy.

"We had a very good time. I got presents, too," I said. "I am going to wear some of them tonight."

"It is time to wash up, everyone," said Nannie. "I would like help getting dinner on the table."

I ran upstairs and put on the new red

sweater and matching socks Mommy had given me for Christmas. Seth had given me a very pretty bracelet made of beads. I put that on, too. Then I ran downstairs again.

Everyone had a job to do. Even Emily. She was putting a spoon at each place.

By the time we finished setting out the food, our big dining-room table was filled up. We were going to have turkey, gravy, stuffing, sweet potatoes, cranberry sauce, green beans, bread, and salad. For dessert, there were three kinds of pie. It was a feast!

"I hope no one is too tired to trim the tree," said Daddy when we finished eating.

"No way!" I replied.

"Ready or not, tree, here we come!" said Andrew.

It was a good thing the tree was big and strong. We hung a lot of ornaments on it. We added lights and tinsel, too.

"It is time to put the angel on top," said Elizabeth. "Sam, will you do that, please?"

Sam climbed up the stepladder and we passed the angel to him.

"Be careful," I said. "She bends easily."

He set the angel gently at the top of the tree.

"She does not look so bad up there," whispered Andrew.

He was right. She was so little we could hardly see her.

"Next year we will get a better angel," I whispered back.

"Let's see how the tree looks all lit up," said Daddy.

He turned off the lights in the room. Then he lit the tree.

"Wow! It is the most beautiful tree we have ever had!" I said.

Everyone agreed. No one seemed to mind our little pipe cleaner angel at the top.

"Come, gather around," said Nannie. "I will read you the story of Christmas."

Nannie read to us from the Bible. My favorite part was when the angel says to the shepherds, "Behold, I bring you good tidings of great joy, which shall be to all people." (I knew that line by heart from the pageant.)

When Nannie finished, Daddy and Elizabeth took turns reading from *A Christmas Carol*. Then we all took turns reading "The Night Before Christmas." (Emily does not read yet. But we taught her to say, "Now dash away! dash away! dash away all!")

We left a delicious snack of milk and cookies for Santa. We hung our stockings. Soon it was time for bed. I closed my eyes. The words to "The Night Before Christmas" were still floating in my head.

'Twas the night before Christmas,
*   when all through the house*
Not a creature was stirring,
*   not even a mouse;*
The stockings were hung
*   by the chimney with care,*
In hopes that St. Nicholas
*   soon would be there.*

I tried to stay awake. I wanted to listen for the sound of sleigh bells ringing. But I could not do it. I fell asleep dreaming that Santa was on his way.

19

Christmas Mystery

"Merry Christmas, Moosie! Merry Christmas, Emily. Merry Christmas, everyone!" I called.

I jumped out of bed on Christmas morning and ran to Andrew's room.

"Merry Christmas, Andrew," I said. "Let's go find Kristy."

Kristy was awake and playing with Emily in Emily's room. David Michael came into the room. Then Sam and Charlie joined us.

"Let's all go downstairs," I said.

"We can't. The grown-ups want us to wait," said Kristy. "They want to light a fire and make coffee and stuff."

"Nannie will announce when we can come down," said Charlie.

"I smell the coffee," I said. "So we may not have to wait too long."

We did not have to wait even one more minute.

"All right, kids. You can come down now," called Nannie.

We raced down the stairs together.

"Merry Christmas!" said Daddy, Elizabeth, and Nannie together.

They had lit a fire so the room was glowing. Santa's midnight snack was gone. Just a little milk was left in his glass and a few cookie crumbs on his plate. Our stockings were stuffed.

I was about to make a run for my stocking when I noticed that something was different about our tree. It was the angel on top. It was not the one we had put there the

night before. It was not the one Andrew and I had tried to buy, either. But she was just as pretty as that one.

"Ooh," I said. "Where did that angel come from?"

Everyone stopped what they were doing and stared up at the tree. They looked just as surprised as I did. Even Sam. He had said there are no such things as angels. But he did not look so sure anymore.

"Where *did* it come from?" asked Kristy.

No one seemed to know. Maybe there really *are* angels. Maybe a real angel brought this one for our tree.

I looked at the angel and smiled. You know what? I think she smiled back.

20

Angels Everywhere

I took down my stocking and unwrapped the goodies inside. I found a little book of puzzles, a pencil with a silly head for an eraser, a pair of mittens with reindeer on them, and two candy canes and a chocolate Santa.

Ting-a-ling. Nannie was standing in the doorway, ringing a silver bell.

"Breakfast is served," she said.

She was wearing a white apron and a Santa hat. Daddy and Elizabeth came out of the kitchen dressed the same way.

"You are not allowed to help with break-fast this morning," said Elizabeth. "The grown-ups are going to serve you."

"All right!" said David Michael.

Another feast was on the table. Fancy napkins and juice glasses had been set out. All we had to do was eat and have fun.

When breakfast was over, Daddy said we were allowed to help again. So we cleaned up together.

Ring, ring. Mommy and Seth called to wish us a merry Christmas.

When we hung up, the phone rang again. It was Neena. She is Daddy's mother. We took turns talking to her. Then Daddy said, "It is time to open the presents under the tree."

Oh, boy! I started reading gift tags, un-tying ribbons, and tearing paper off pack-ages. I got the best, most thoughtful gifts. I got books and games and clothes. Some of my presents were store-bought. Some were homemade. I got some envelopes from relatives with cards and money, too.

I thanked everyone and they thanked me. I was happy they liked the gifts I gave them.

Ding-dong. Hannie and Linny were at the door. They visited for awhile. Then Andrew, David Michael, and I went to their house.

We spent the day eating, visiting, and talking on the phone. Just before dinner, it started to snow again. I ran outside and made a snow angel again. Then another. And another. By the time I finished, there were angels all over the yard. I thought they would be good company for the angel on our Christmas tree.

I got wet making all those angels. So I went inside to change my clothes. It was almost time for dinner anyway.

We ate some very delicious leftovers. Then we sat around the fire and talked and read until it was time for bed.

Before I went to sleep, I lined up my gifts to look at them. I counted the money I had received. There was a lot. I knew one important thing I would do with the money.

I went to Andrew's room. He was still awake.

"How much money did you get for Christmas?" I asked.

"I do not know," he replied. "I could not count it."

I counted it for him. He had a lot.

"We have enough to pay Daddy back and still have some left over," I said.

We agreed we would give the money to Daddy first thing in the morning. Then I went back to my room.

"It was a perfect Christmas, Moosie," I said. "And a mysterious one, too."

I thought about the angels in the yard. And I thought about the angel on top of the tree. There were angels everywhere.

I guess I would never know where the angel on the tree came from. But I was glad she was there to watch over me.

About the Author

ANN M. MARTIN lives in New York City and loves animals, especially cats. She has a cat of her own, Gussie.

Other books by Ann M. Martin that you might enjoy are *Stage Fright; Me and Katie (the Pest)*; and the books in *The Baby-sitters Club* series.

Ann likes ice cream and *I Love Lucy*. And she has her own little sister, whose name is Jane.

Little Sister

Don't miss #69

KAREN'S BIG SISTER

"Karen Brewer! How can you say something like that? You really hurt my feelings," said Kristy. "After all this time, how can you still think that way? I thought we were close. I thought we were family. *Real* family."

"Well you hurt my feelings, too," I said. "Real family lend each other things. I do not see why you will not lend me the pin."

"You know I lend you things all the time," said Kristy. "I explained my reasons for not wanting to lend you this pin. It would be nice if you were more understanding about it."

"Well, I do not understand," I replied. "Not at all."

I walked out of Kristy's room in a huff and went to bed. I was so mad.

LITTLE APPLE®

BABY-SITTERS

Little Sister™
by Ann M. Martin, author of *The Baby-sitters Club*®

☐ MQ44300-3 #1	Karen's Witch	$2.95
☐ MQ44259-7 #2	Karen's Roller Skates	$2.95
☐ MQ44299-7 #3	Karen's Worst Day	$2.95
☐ MQ44264-3 #4	Karen's Kittycat Club	$2.95
☐ MQ44258-9 #5	Karen's School Picture	$2.95
☐ MQ44298-8 #6	Karen's Little Sister	$2.95
☐ MQ44257-0 #7	Karen's Birthday	$2.95
☐ MQ42670-2 #8	Karen's Haircut	$2.95
☐ MQ43652-X #9	Karen's Sleepover	$2.95
☐ MQ43651-1 #10	Karen's Grandmothers	$2.95
☐ MQ43650-3 #11	Karen's Prize	$2.95
☐ MQ43649-X #12	Karen's Ghost	$2.95
☐ MQ43648-1 #13	Karen's Surprise	$2.95
☐ MQ43646-5 #14	Karen's New Year	$2.95
☐ MQ43645-7 #15	Karen's in Love	$2.95
☐ MQ43644-9 #16	Karen's Goldfish	$2.95
☐ MQ43643-0 #17	Karen's Brothers	$2.95
☐ MQ43642-2 #18	Karen's Home Run	$2.95
☐ MQ43641-4 #19	Karen's Good-Bye	$2.95
☐ MQ44823-4 #20	Karen's Carnival	$2.95
☐ MQ44824-2 #21	Karen's New Teacher	$2.95
☐ MQ44833-1 #22	Karen's Little Witch	$2.95
☐ MQ44832-3 #23	Karen's Doll	$2.95
☐ MQ44859-5 #24	Karen's School Trip	$2.95
☐ MQ44831-5 #25	Karen's Pen Pal	$2.95
☐ MQ44830-7 #26	Karen's Ducklings	$2.75
☐ MQ44829-3 #27	Karen's Big Joke	$2.95
☐ MQ44828-5 #28	Karen's Tea Party	$2.95
☐ MQ44825-0 #29	Karen's Cartwheel	$2.75
☐ MQ45645-8 #30	Karen's Kittens	$2.95
☐ MQ45646-6 #31	Karen's Bully	$2.95
☐ MQ45647-4 #32	Karen's Pumpkin Patch	$2.95
☐ MQ45648-2 #33	Karen's Secret	$2.95
☐ MQ45650-4 #34	Karen's Snow Day	$2.95
☐ MQ45652-0 #35	Karen's Doll Hospital	$2.95
☐ MQ45651-2 #36	Karen's New Friend	$2.95
☐ MQ45653-9 #37	Karen's Tuba	$2.95
☐ MQ45655-5 #38	Karen's Big Lie	$2.95
☐ MQ45654-7 #39	Karen's Wedding	$2.95
☐ MQ47040-X #40	Karen's Newspaper	$2.95

More Titles... ➡

The Baby-sitters Little Sister titles continued...

Available wherever you buy books, or use this order form.

Now THE BABY-SITTERS CLUB®

★ is a Video Club too! ★